TREEHOUSE TOWN

Illustrated by McKenzie Rose West | Written by Jenny Phillips

BOOK 1

Written by Jenny Phillips
Illustrated by McKenzie Rose West
Cover Design by Elle Staples

goodandbeautiful.com

CHAPTER 1

In a big green valley, there was a nice little forest. Three homes sat snugly in it.

In the yellow home lived Jake and his family. Jake had two little twin sisters and a spotted dog named Chase.

In the white home lived Ella, her little brother, and her parents. Ella had a little white cat that wore a gold bell.

The other home was empty. No one lived there.

A lonely "For Sale" sign blew in the breeze.

The "For Sale" sign had been there for a long time.

Sadly, no one took care of the empty home.

The yard was full of prickly weeds.

Each window was dirty.

Paint was peeling off the door and the side of the home.

All the shutters were broken.

Jake and Ella were best friends. They often rode their bikes past the empty house.

They loved to explore the
forest behind their homes.
They saw squirrels.

They heard birds.

They smelled pine needles
and flowers and the fresh,
clean dirt.

CHAPTER 2

One fine day in early fall, Jake and Ella rode past the empty house. Jake suddenly stopped.

"Look!" he shouted as he pointed to the house. "There is a nice pot of flowers on the porch."

"That was not there before," said Ella. "I wonder who put it there."

The kids looked in the
windows. The home looked
as empty as ever.

Jake's and Ella's parents did not know who put the flowers on the porch. No one knew. It was a mystery.

Jake and Ella stopped often and sat on the porch by the flowers, smelling them. No matter how long they waited, however, they never saw anyone, but Ella noticed that the flowers were always watered.

"This *is* a mystery!" said Ella.

A few days later, the two friends discovered another mystery.

They were walking through the forest in a part they did not visit often. The ground was soft with moss. It had rained the night before, and the air smelled fresh.

Ella heard a squirrel in the tree above her. She looked up and saw something.

"Look, Jake!"

There, high in the tree, was a piece of rope hanging from a tree limb. At the end of the rope was a silver bucket.

The children ran to Ella's home as fast as they could. Her dad worked from home. They told him about the rope and the bucket.

"Wait until my break," he said, "and I will come see it."

An hour later, they were all walking into the forest, Ella's dad carrying a long ladder.

Finally, they reached the spot, and Ella's dad went up the ladder, disappearing into the leaves.

"Oh, children!" he cried.
"You'll never believe what is
up here! There is a huge, very
well-built tree fort. Someone

who used to live in one of these houses must have built it. It would take some work, but we could restore it and build a safe ladder to go up the tree."

"Oh, Dad!" cried Ella. "That would be wonderful!"

The children clapped their hands.

CHAPTER 3

As Ella and Jake worked on the treehouse with their fathers, they discovered that the treehouse had been built to look like an old, one-room schoolhouse.

They found a gold bell on the roof and polished it. They sanded the wood walls until they were smooth and then painted them red. They built a sturdy ladder. They tied the silver bucket to a new, strong rope and rigged it so that they could easily pull it up and down.

Ella's father built a bookcase, and Ella's mother filled it with books.

Jake's father built a few desks, and Jake's mother filled them with school supplies.

Jake and Ella gathered money they had saved and bought a big chalkboard. The fathers helped install it at the front of the room.

The treehouse was done!

Ella and Jake loved playing school in the treehouse. They took turns being the teacher and invited Ella's five-year-old brother and Jake's six-year-old twin sisters to be the students.

Math was Jake's favorite subject to teach, and art was Ella's favorite subject to teach.

One evening, Ella was sitting on her back porch with her little brother, Wesley. A lantern gave enough light for Ella to see the hook rug she was making for the treehouse.

Suddenly, Wesley stood up, pointed to the woods, and shouted, "What's that light?"

Sure enough, Ella could see a bright light shining from the forest. The two siblings ran inside to tell their parents,

but when the parents ran out
to the porch, the light was
gone.

"It was really there!"
exclaimed Ella.

"I believe you," said her
father. "We'll keep an eye
out to see if it comes back. I
wonder what it could be."

Ella and Jake found more
odd things the next day.
When they went to see how
the flowers were doing on
the porch of the empty house,

Jake noticed something.

"Hey! The 'For Sale' sign is gone."

"You're right!" agreed Ella. "And look! The windows are no longer dirty, and the shutters have been painted."

The two children knocked on the door, deciding to welcome the new neighbors. No one answered. Ella noticed two more big pots of beautiful plants on the porch.

"Let's wait for them," suggested Ella. "Let's wait,

even if it takes all day."

The two children had packed books and lunches for playing in the treehouse. Instead, they sat on the front porch of the home and read and ate and waited. Chase, the dog, sat with them too.

No one came out of the house. No one went into the house. The house stood silent and apparently empty.

The mailman came by and dropped a package into the mailbox. It was so big that he couldn't shut the mailbox.

No one came out to get the package.

Finally, when the sun started to sink lower in the sky, Ella and Jake went home, discouraged and confused.

As Ella lay in her bed, she thought of the light in the forest, the clean windows, and the package in the mailbox. She had an idea. "I'm going to get up early," she said, "and go check something. I think it will give me a clue."

CHAPTER 4

As the early morning sunlight poured into the valley, Ella rode as fast as she could to the empty home.

She skidded to a stop in
front of the mailbox, and her
eyes grew big. The package
was no longer in the mailbox.

Like a tornado, she sped
to Jake's house and tapped
on his window. Sleepily, Jake
opened the window.

"The package in the mailbox
is gone!" cried Ella.

The two children, however,
had no idea how to solve the
mystery about the empty

house. They decided to give it a break and go swimming after they finished their chores.

Ella's mom loved to take the children swimming. She laid out a blanket on the grassy river bank in the shade of a

big tree and read books while the children swam.

She always packed a delicious lunch. She always pointed out the sounds of the birds, the breeze, and the rustling leaves. Ella thought her mom was amazing.

As the group was walking home, Chase suddenly lifted his head, let out a little bark, and shot off into the forest like an arrow.

"Chase!" cried Jake. "Come back!"

But Chase didn't come back, and Ella and Jake took off into the forest to follow Chase.

It was not at all like Chase to run off like that.

Finally, the children caught

up with Chase. He was
whining at a group of big
bushes at the base of a big
tree close to the schoolhouse
treehouse.

"Listen," said Ella. "I hear something."

A faint meowing sound came from the bushes.

"It sounds like Snow!" cried Ella, thinking of her little white cat as she and Jake started looking in the bushes.

As they parted the tall bushes, they found Snow with her leg tangled in a rope. Quickly, Ella untangled Snow's leg and held her gently. The cat seemed fine.

"Ella!" shouted Jake, who

was still looking in the bushes.
"There is something in these
bushes—something big and
made of wood."

Ella and Jake explored the
bushes until they realized
what the thing was—another
treehouse! This one had been
built very low in the tree. It
had a little ramp that led up to
it. It was Jake who first found
the faded words painted on
the front: BAKERY.

CHAPTER 5

That evening, Ella and Jake and their fathers walked through the forest on the way to the new treehouse. Ella looked ahead of her at the scene. Sunlight slanted through the trees and lit up a few yellow leaves that floated quietly to the ground. Moss dotted the tree trunks. It was beautiful.

"A bakery treehouse!" said Ella's father as they walked. "You know that my grandfather owned this property. I never came here when he was alive because I lived in Spain when I was a child. My parents never mentioned treehouses on this land, but no one ever lived here except my grandfather."

"It sounds like another mystery," said Ella. "I wonder why your grandfather would have built them."

"Me too," replied her father as they arrived at the new treehouse. "Here we are. I will start cutting away the bushes. The rest of you can go in the treehouse and start cleaning it up."

Three days later, the treehouse had a complete makeover. The bushes were gone, revealing a beautiful blue-and-white treehouse close to the ground.

The inside of the treehouse had display shelves, a small kitchen area, and a checkout counter.

"It's amazing!" said Jake.

"Yes, it is," agreed Ella. "I wish we had some things to

put in it, like cookie cutters."
The kids and their parents
had spent all their extra
money buying things for
the schoolhouse treehouse
and paint for the bakery
treehouse.

"We'll have to save up our money," said Jake. "For now, let's go in and pretend we are making cookies."

"And cake and doughnuts," added Ella.

The next day, Ella and Jake were chatting happily when they arrived at the bakery treehouse. They suddenly stopped when they saw a neatly wrapped package with a blue ribbon on the ramp of the treehouse.

A little tag on the package read:

For your new treehouse.

  From,

  The Two Ts

Neither Jake nor Ella knew who "The Two Ts" were, but they opened the package and, to their delight, discovered a set of cookie cutters and a wooden rolling pin with red handles.

"All right!" said Ella. "There are too many mysteries. First, the empty house. Second, the light in the forest I sometimes see at night. Third, this package!"

"I know," said Jake. "These are such nice gifts. I wonder who 'The Two Ts' are."

"Let's leave a note," said Ella.

Dear Two Ts,

Thank you very much for your gifts.

We love them. Who are you?

Ella and Jake hurried home
to tell their parents about the
new gifts.

The next day, a note
was pinned to the bakery
treehouse door:

We are your treehouse neighbors. Here
is a map to our treehouse. It's not far.

CHAPTER 6

Ella and Jake raced home, flying like deer through the forest. Both of their dads agreed to go find the treehouse with them.

Carefully, they followed the map, which was easy to read. Finally, they walked into an open clearing and saw a beautiful treehouse with the words **FLOWER SHOP** painted on it.

The group stood in total silence as they took in the beautiful sight of the treehouse. Their minds raced with questions.

"You know," said Ella's dad, "the land that this treehouse

is on belongs to the empty

house."

"Oh!" said Ella. "I thought

of something else, too. This

seems to be right where the

light in the forest was coming

from. Whoever built this

treehouse probably built it at night."

"But why?" asked Jake.

The question hung in the air. No one had an answer.

The treehouse was empty, just as empty as the house.

The next morning, Jake and Ella and Ella's dad biked to the empty home. It was all fixed up now. The yard looked wonderful. The shutters were repaired. The house was painted. The weeds were gone from the lawn.

Ella noticed something else. "There is smoke coming out of the chimney!"

"You're right!" exclaimed Jake. "Let's knock on the door. Someone must be here!"

The children rushed up to the porch. Ella's dad followed. Before they knocked, they listened. A piano was being played inside. Then they heard laughter from another part of the house. People were there! The empty house was no longer empty.

With excitement pounding in her heart, Ella knocked loudly on the door.

There was a sound of pattering footsteps. Then the

door slowly opened. There
stood a boy and a girl about
Ella and Jake's age.

The girl and the boy stared
shyly at the visitors. The girl

had straight, glossy black hair that almost went to her chin. The boy also had straight, dark hair.

"We came to welcome you," said Jake. "I'm Jake, and this is my friend, Ella, and her dad. We live in the other two houses that border the forest. Did you just move in?"

"Kind of," said the boy. "I'm Thomas, and this is my sister, Tori. We're twins."

"Wait!" Ella yelled. Then she

blushed and said quietly, "Are you 'The Two Ts'?"

"Yes!" said Tori. "You must own the other two treehouses."

"Yes, we do!" said Ella.

"How did you ever think of building a schoolhouse treehouse and a bakery treehouse?"

"We didn't," said Jake. "We think Ella's grandfather did. He used to own all of this land, and he lived on it ever since he was a baby. It must have been him, but we don't know *why* he built them."

"I love your flower shop treehouse," said Ella.

"Thank you!" said Tori. "I want to own a real flower shop someday. The pots of flowers on the porch are mine."

"But how did they get here? There has been no one in the house."

"Oh, we've been here," said Thomas. "Come see our swing

in the backyard, and we'll tell you everything."

Ella's dad talked to Thomas and Tori's dad while the four children sat on the swings as Thomas explained.

"We bought the house months ago, but we couldn't move in yet because my dad was finishing his job in the city. Plus, this old house needed some work before we could move in. Many days after work, we would drive out here."

"From the city?" asked Ella. "That's a long drive."

"Yes," said Thomas, "but it is a beautiful drive. We always arrived at the house just before it got dark.

"We slept in sleeping bags while our dad worked until late at night, repairing the house. He has a very strong set of lights. Since our house is so far away from anyone else, the noise and lights didn't bother anyone."

"Did your father build the flower shop treehouse?"

"Yes. On a couple of evenings, before it got dark, we hurried and explored the forest and found your treehouses. Tori said, 'Oh, if

I were to have a treehouse,
I would have a flower shop
treehouse.' She was so excited
about it that Dad decided to
build it for her. He had to do it
at night, though, after she fell
asleep. He built it as close to
yours as he could while still
being on our land. He thought
we could eventually build a
whole town of treehouses.
He's a carpenter, you know.
He's done with his city job,
and he works from home
now, building furniture in the

old barn behind our house."

"Well!" said Ella with a long sigh. "That explains a lot. We're glad you're here!"

"We are, too!" said Tori.

"Do you want to head to the

treehouse town?" asked Jake.

All four of the children jumped up, asked their dads, and in no time, they were sailing across the road on their bikes in the cool fall air.

Try a Level 3* Book from
The Good and the Beautiful Library

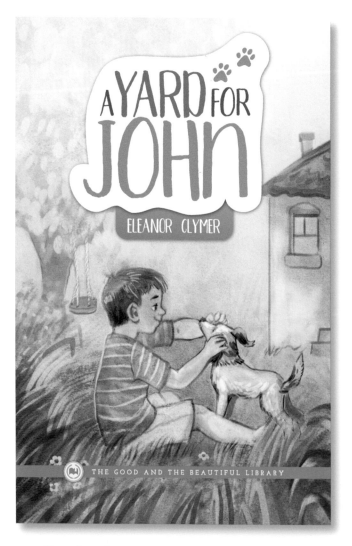

A YARD FOR JOHN

ELEANOR CLYMER

THE GOOD AND THE BEAUTIFUL LIBRARY

*Reading level assessment is available at
goodandbeautiful.com

Here's Another Level 3 Book from
The Good and the Beautiful Library*

Freddy
AND
Linda

THE GOOD AND THE BEAUTIFUL LIBRARY

Jane Quigg

*Reading level assessment is available at
goodandbeautiful.com*

Here's Another Level 3* Book from
The Good and the Beautiful Library

*Reading level assessment is available at
goodandbeautiful.com